Pippa
Goodhart

esley
Danson

Dragon Magic

For everyone at
Swanbourne House School
P.G.

For Jack, Bill and Ted
L.D.

EGMONT
We bring stories to life

First published in Great Britain 2009
by Egmont UK Ltd
239 Kensington High Street, London W8 6SA
Text copyright © Pippa Goodhart 2009
Illustrations copyright © Lesley Danson 2009
The author and illustrator have asserted their moral rights.
ISBN 978 1 4052 4611 8
10 9 8 7 6 5 4 3 2 1
A CIP catalogue record for this title is available from the British Library.
Printed in Singapore.

Contents

Red Bananas

Huff and the Blacksmith

Jess's dad was Big John the blacksmith. Huff
the dragon blew fire to soften the iron so that
Big John could work it. Bang, bang, clang,
clang clang! But Huff was old and his fire was
growing dim. So Big John could only work
slowly.

Big John was making a gate for the King.
It was a gate that drew pictures in the air. Big
John had made the bottom part of the gate in
shapes of waves and fishes.

Huff blew a smudge of smoke and out came
a flicker of fire.

'Quick, Dad!' said Jess. 'There's some fire!'

Big John put a very small bit of metal into Huff's fire and he worked fast, hammering and twisting and tweaking.

What is it?

'What's that bit going to be?' asked Jess.

'A flower,' said Big John. 'This part of the gate is going to be a meadow.'

'It's beautiful!' said Jess. 'Could you put a mouse on its stalk?'

'Hmm,' said Big John. 'I can if Huff can blow enough fire.' Big John patted Huff's head. 'Have you any more fire for me today, Huff?' Huff blinked tired eyes. His fire had gone.

Big John sighed. 'We really need a new young dragon to help with the work.'

'Where do dragons come from?' asked Jess.

'I got Huff from a dragon merchant wizard, long ago on my travels,' said Big John. 'He knew exactly the kind of dragon for me. But I couldn't travel and find that wizard now.'

9

'I could go and look for him!' said Jess.

'You're too young to go exploring the world on your own,' said Big John. He sighed. 'I think that I shall just have to give up being a blacksmith once this gate is finished.'

'No!' said Jess. 'I'll ask the King if he can help us. Wait here!' And off she ran.

10

A Dragon from the King

I hope the King is in.

Jess knocked on the palace door.

'Please, Your Majesty,' said Jess. 'Do you know how we could get a dragon without finding a wizard? We need a new dragon to help make your gate.'

11

'Oh dear, isn't the gate finished yet?' said the King. 'I can't help worrying. Anybody could come into the town while there is no gate to close the hole in the wall. Tell your father that he must hurry and finish it fast.'

'He can't do it fast without a new dragon. Poor old Huff hasn't got much fire nowadays,' said Jess.

'Oh,' said the King. 'Um,' said the King.
'Well, we do have some dragon eggs in the
palace museum. I wonder if they would still
hatch if they were warmed and charmed?
Come with me.'

13

The King
uncovered a case
full of eggs.
They glowed with
magical life.

'What kind of
dragons are in these
eggs?' asked Jess.

'Er,' said the King. 'I don't really know. We
seem to have lost the labels.'

So Jess just had to guess which egg to take.
She touched them all, and one of them gave
a fuzzy feeling back.

'Please could I
have this one?' she
said. 'I just hope
that it's a friendly
and firey kind of
dragon.'

Hatching Puff

Huff sniffed the dragon egg. He tucked his little wing over it and he sang a strange lullaby kind of noise to it.

'Huff's hot breath will warm the egg,' said Big John. 'And his song will charm it. I wonder how long it will take to hatch?'

Jess kept checking on the egg. On the third day she shouted, 'It's got a crack! Dad, come and see!'

They watched the crack zig-zag around the egg.

The shell fell apart and there, in a kind of glow, sat a little dragon chick.

'It's red!' said Jess. She reached out a finger to touch, and the baby dragon sneezed. A tiny spark came out from its nose.

'It does breathe fire!' said Big John. 'Well done, Jess and Huff!'

'Let's call her Puff,' said Jess. 'I'll make her a bed, and I'll give her milk and mustard to drink. And Huff can sing his dragon songs to her.'

Puff Begins to Fire

Puff grew fast. She began to flap her wings and breathe proper fire. Huff steered Puff away from breathing fire on the furniture. Huff and Jess took Puff out to the meadow, and Puff stretched her wings.

'Are you a flying kind of dragon?' asked Jess.

Puff flapped her wings. She began to lift into the air. She flew around, snorting excited sparks, and smiling.

'Oh, Puff, come back!' called Jess. Jess shaded her eyes. 'Puff!'

Old Huff raised his head up and he made a charming sound that Jess had never heard him make before. It was a magical

sound, rich and round, and it called out to Puff. Puff paused, up in the sky.

'Come back, Puff!' said Jess once more, and Puff did.

20

'Oh, Puff!' Jess hugged Puff. 'Please don't do that again!' Jess kept her hand on Puff's back as they walked back to the forge.

Good girl, Puff.

'Cheer up, Puff!' said Jess. 'Dad will let you work the iron with him soon!'

When they got home, Jess toasted crumpets in Puff's firey breath. Puff kept the flame steady and not too strong. She smiled when Jess patted her and told her how clever she was, but she didn't want any crumpet.

'I think Puff's ready to try a bit of iron mongery,' said Big John. 'Shall we see if we can make a dragon to stand among the flowers?'

But just then there came a loud noise from
outside the forge.

"It's the King's trumpet!" said Big John.

Strangers are Coming!

The King hurried into the forge, then stopped still when he saw the dragons.

'Your Majesty!' said Big John, wiping his hand on his leather apron. 'What can I do for you?'

'Big John, you have to save us!' said the King.

Big John frowned. 'Save us from what, Your Majesty?'

'Strangers!' said the King. 'A horde of strangers carrying sticks! They're coming up the mountain, heading this way! And there is no gate to stop them!'

Are you sure?

Big John stroked his chin. 'Do we know why these people are coming?'

'Who knows?' wailed the King. 'To attack? To steal? To take our children? They might do anything! Anything!'

'Sit down,' Jess told the King. 'Breathe slowly. Calm down.' The King sat, but he went on fussing.

'You must finish the gate at once!' he said. 'Make the gate solid and strong to keep the strangers out!'

'If Puff can manage it, we will finish the gate tonight,' said Big John. 'It will be strong enough to keep us all safe.'

Off went the King.

'The King wants a solid gate, and we're making a gate that's full of holes!' said Jess, stroking Huff and Puff's heads.

'Don't you worry,' said Big John. 'Give Puff some extra mustard in her feed, Jess. She's going to have to work hard.'

Making the Gate

Big John set to work. Huff showed Puff how to blow the fire where Big John wanted it.

'Come on, little Puff!' said Big John. 'You've got a very important job to do!'

Puff blew great magical flames of orange-yellow fire. She was enjoying it. Big John held rods of iron in large tongs, brightening and softening the iron in the flames. Bang, bang, clang, clang, clang! He worked the iron on

his anvil, hammering and twisting and welding the metal. Then he dipped the hot metal into a trough of water to hiss and steam and harden. Before picking up another rod and starting again. Bang, bang, clang, clang, clang!

Jess polished Puff's
scales with an oily rag
to rub off the soot.
She fed Puff on
ginger and chillies
and mustard milk.
'Good girl,' she
said. 'Well done,
Puff.' But Puff was
getting tired. She
hardly looked at the food.
Her head drooped,
but she went
on blowing
her magical
fire for the
blacksmith.
    'Poor Puff,'
said Jess.

They worked on as the sky grew dark. They worked on as the sky went pink with morning light. Jess was worried.

'Dad, Puff doesn't look well!'

Puff's eyes had lost their sparkle. She could hardly stand.

Are you ill?

'Poor Puff,' said Big John. 'But we're nearly finished.'

The Strangers are Here!

'The strangers are almost here!' shouted
the King, hurrying along the lane.

Jess told him, 'Dad's finished the gate. Look!'

But,

'OH!' said the King and the people.

The gate drew with metal lines in the air dragons and a river and fishes and flowers and trees and animals and birds and insects.

'NO!' wailed the King. 'Oh, no, no, NO! That gate is full of holes! I told you to make a strong gate!'

'It's the holes that make this gate strong,' said Big John. 'This is a gate made with dragon magic. Put it in place, and you will see how it works.'

They hung the gate. Big John waited with the King.

The King pulled out his sword.

'That won't be needed,' said Big John.

'But they have sticks!' said the King.

'Walking sticks to help them climb the mountain,' said Big John.

Just then, Jess came running from the forge. 'Dad, Puff is really ill! She can hardly breathe! Huff is singing, but . . .'

Just at that moment the strangers arrived, there, on the other side of the gate.

With a shaking voice, the King asked the strangers, 'Wh–what do you want from us?' But the strangers weren't looking at the King. They were looking at the gate.

'Oh, it's beautiful!' they said.

'Look, there's a Mountain Dragon!' said a boy, pointing.

'That's Huff,' Jess told him.

'And that one is a very rare Sea Dragon,' said the boy, pointing to another metal shape.

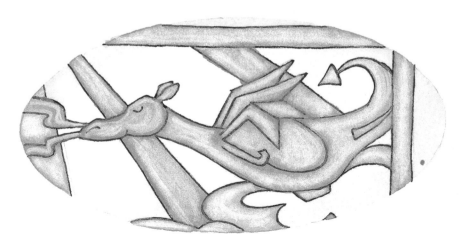

'That's Puff,' said Jess, and the boy told her, 'We saw a Sea Dragon flying over your town, so we've come to look at it.'

'I didn't know she was a Sea Dragon,' said Jess.

'Is she red?' asked the boy.

'She was,' said Jess. 'But she's gone pale now. She's ill.'

'I expect she needs red snappers to eat,' said the boy. 'I've got some in my bundle.'

'Oh, please come quickly and give Puff your fish,' said Jess. She began to turn the key in the gate.

'Oh, dear!' said the King. 'Oh dear, oh dear!'

But Big John told him, 'Put that sword away and help open the gate!'

The King did as he was told.

Rescue for Puff

They swung open the gate, and all the strangers walked into the town.

'We've brought you presents of food,' said the strangers. 'We wanted to see your dragon, but we wanted to meet you too.'

'You are most welcome,' said Big John.

Jess ran with the boy to the forge.

'Puff is in here. Oh, look! I think she's dying!'

Puff could hardly lift her head or open her eyes.

The boy took red snapper fish from his bag. Jess could smell the tang of the sea from the fish.

So could Puff.
Her ears went up.
Her nose sniffed.
She licked the fish.

Then she did lift her head. She opened her

mouth and she gobbled the fish down.

'Oh, thank goodness!' smiled Jess.

'A Sea Dragon needs sea fish,' said the boy.

As Puff ate, her red colour came back. She got to her feet. She puffed some fire, then she looked up at the sky.

Hooray!

'She needs to fly,' said the boy. 'Red Sea Dragons catch fish by flying over the sea, diving and fishing as they go.'

'But I can't let her fly away!' said Jess.

'Then ride her,' said the boy.

Friends

So Jess and the boy and Puff went flying. They flew over the town where a party was happening. They flew down the mountain, over to the town where the boy lived, to the sea. They flew over the sea, swooping down to catch red snapper fish. Then they flew back up the mountain, taking fish for the party.

'You can fly people down to the sea to visit us,' said the boy. 'And I want to stay with you and learn how to be a blacksmith just like Big John.'

So that's what happened. Jess became a blacksmith too. And Puff had baby dragons who all flew and all breathed fire.